A Search for Purpose

A Novella

MJ Jennetti

Disclaimer

The story, all names, characters, and incidents portrayed in this book are fictitious. No identification with actual persons (living or deceased), places, buildings, and products is intended or should be inferred.

"For my husband, Tony, and daughter, Theresa, and for all people with disabilities

Table of Contents

"To everything there is a season, and   a time to every purpose under heaven."

From Ecclesiastes

PART 1

A Search for Purpose

Trent

I t's early June, 1994, in the small town of Rhodes a few miles outside of Sacramento in the Central Valley of California. Already it's unseasonably warm for this time of year. Temperatures can reach well over 100 degrees in the summer, while in the winter dense fog can coat the area making driving very hazardous. Many horrendous pileups have occurred during these times when drivers refuse to slow down even though they can't see but a few feet ahead of them. More than one citizen of Rhodes has lost a loved one this way.

Rhodes has a population of just over 9000. There is only one rather rundown movie theater, one main grocery along with a couple of mom-and-pop stores, a couple of gas stations, a hardware store, several churches and too many bars. There are no museums, art galleries or symphony orchestra. Rhodes is mostly a blue-collar town. Most vote Republican, always have and always will.

Trent Harding's family has been in Rhodes for several generations. His grandparents migrated here from Nebraska in the 1920s hoping to escape the terrible winters, never having regretted their decision. Trent's father Duane is a highly skilled auto mechanic whose services are always in demand. His mother Carol stays at home to run the household and look after Trent's younger brother Davy who has Down's syndrome. Duane is a rather heavy- set man with a bit of a paunch. He always has grease on his hands from working on vehicles. Carol is petite and attractive. Theirs is a very traditional household in the old sense where Duane manages all of the finances of which Carol is left pretty much in the dark. However, she worries how she would manage if she were ever left on her own.

Trent has always resented 16-year- old Davy feeling that his parents favored Davy over him. Granted they were very proud of Trent's accomplishments. He has just been voted valedictorian of his senior class and was captain of the Bears football team, but they always seemed to put Davy first. Trent was also ashamed of having a brother with Down's syndrome. Consequently, he preferred to go to his friends' homes rather than have them come to his. Not many of them even know that Davy exists, and Trent wanted to keep it that way. Trent was looking forward to going away to college in the fall. He had been accepted to UCLA on a football scholarship and saw it as a way to escape his family and forget about Davy once and for all. He took pride in being a handsome six-foot-tall young man with a thick head of light brown hair, vivid blue eyes and a flawless complexion. Many of his female classmates had a crush on him, but Trent only had eyes for his girlfriend Sally Davis whom he had dated throughout high school.

Sally was petite and barely came to Trent's shoulder. For this they were nicknamed Mutt and Jeff and took it in stride. Sally had blond hair the color of corn silk which hung just to the top of her shoulders, and she had the same blue eyes as Trent. However, unlike Trent, Sally was not planning to attend college. She wanted to study cosmetology and eventually become a hair dresser. She hoped to one day have a salon of her own, as she felt she had a knack for business. Time would tell if she and Trent could maintain a long-distance relationship. Duane and Carol liked Sally. Her parents were devout Christians like they were. Sally's father Mitch worked at the local hardware store, and her mother Linda was a hairdresser. That's why Sally had taken an interest in doing the same.

Sally had made it clear to Trent that she was not interested in having sex before marriage. Even though Trent did not agree, he was willing to accept Sally's wishes in the hope that they would one day marry. He couldn't envision himself with anyone else. They would have the summer and later on the holidays together, and Trent was already looking forward to them. He especially loved Christmas, putting up the tree and other decorations. Every year he and Duane would hang colored lights across the front of their place. He always wished it would snow, but that was highly unlikely in Rhodes. Once in a while there was a light dusting of snow, but it would melt very quickly.

It is the morning of the graduation ceremony which thankfully will take place in the high school gymnasium which is air-conditioned. The temperature is already in the high 80's, and it would be sweltering sitting outside in all this heat. Trent is just finishing breakfast and plans to meet Sally before the ceremony.

"I don't like the idea of you riding your motorcycle there," said Carol.

His parents had given the motorcycle to Trent

on his 16th birthday instead of giving him a car. Duane thought it would be far cheaper to drive and maintain than a car and didn't feel there was that much traffic going through town. Carol finally relented, but she didn't feel that good about it.

"Just be sure and wear your helmet," Carol cautioned. "Don't I always. You don't have to keep reminding me over and over."

Carol knew she hounded Trent more often than she should, but she couldn't help herself. She would never forgive herself if anything ever happened to Trent, nor would she ever forgive Duane.

Trent went out to board his motorcycle, draping his graduation gown over the back of it. He was dressed in a pair of shorts with a light weight T-shirt underneath it, judging it was too hot to wear anything else. Sally was waiting for him next to the gymnasium wearing her cap and gown. Trent put his arm around her and kissed her.

"Happy graduation day, babe," said Trent.

"Can't wait to hear your speech," said Sally. "Don't expect anything great," replied Trent. "Well, it will be great to me," said Sally.

They walked arm-and-arm into the gym to cool off before the ceremony which was due to start in an hour. Already others from their class were arriving.

Back home at the Harding household, Duane, Carol and Davy were about to set out themselves. Carol was wearing a colorful print sundress. She was still a beautiful woman, and Duane took pride in being seen with her. Theirs was not a perfect marriage, but then again how many are? Last year they had celebrated their 20th anniversary which was indeed a milestone. However, Carol resented that Duane had to work that day and did not take her to someplace special. She felt he just took her for granted, and she longed for more romance in their marriage. He was no longer the slim handsome man she once knew. Duane didn't make love to her all that often, and he never brought her flowers.

Gradually her resentment had built up over time, and she even considered leaving Duane, but she knew she had no way to support herself on her own. Thus, she felt trapped in a loveless marriage of which Duane seemed to have no clue.

When they arrived at the gym, they found seats near the front. Trent ignored them as he didn't want to be seen with Davy. Hopefully that wouldn't happen after the ceremony. He wanted to leave with Sally as quickly as possible. The graduates were all seated, and after Trent gave his valedictory speech, they all filed up one by one to receive their diplomas. Afterwards they threw their caps in the air and began cheering. Trent realized it would be impossible for him to leave without greeting his family. He was ashamed to see Davy with his large tongue hanging out and ignored him completely. Duane and Carol said how proud they were of him and knew he had a great future ahead of him at UCLA this fall. As soon as Sally came up to see everyone, she and Trent made a quick exit.

"How about we go out for pizza tonight?" said Trent. "Sounds perfect. I couldn't be prouder of you.

I'm glad we still have the whole summer to spend together before you have to head off to college."

"We definitely will make the best of it," replied Trent.

Right now, college seemed a ways off. Time goes more slowly when one is young. It only speeds up the older you get. Trent will look back on this time and wonder where the years went.

Trent and Sally arrived at Jake's Pizza around seven that night and ordered a deluxe pepperoni pizza. The place was not that crowded, and they looked forward to having a chance to talk. Sally had something she wanted to discuss with Trent.

"You know you shouldn't be ashamed of having

Davy as your brother," she said. "I know you have always felt that you came in second to Davy, and that's understandable. It must be difficult for any parent with a disabled child. It's only natural for that child to need extra help. You are not disabled, Trent; you are far from it. They know you will always be able to succeed and take care of yourself. That's not the case with Davy. He will never be able to live on his own, and I'm sure your parents must worry about what will happen to him once they are gone, especially if they feel you will never step up to the plate and look out for him. Try to place yourself in their shoes and know how difficult this must be for them."

"Maybe you are right," said Trent. "Maybe I have been too hard on them. It's just that it's so difficult being in my situation. I've never really discussed this with them, and perhaps I should instead of just lashing out."

"I agree. Maybe this is a way of mending fences

and letting you have a better relationship with your parents.

I don't know what I would do if I had a bad relationship with mine," said Sally. "My parents mean everything to me."

Afterwards they took a walk to the park and sat on a bench holding hands and admiring the full moon. It was a golden orb in the sky, having just appeared above the horizon. It was finally starting to cool down a bit, and there was a slight breeze as well. Sitting there in the park it seemed like nothing could ever go wrong, and the future looked filled with promise for both of them. They were young and in love and felt immortal. How could anything ever change?

The next day Trent decided to make good on having a talk with his parents about his feelings towards them and how they seemed to favor Davy over him. Sally was right, he should bring it out into the open and clear the air once and for all before he

13

left for college in the fall.

"I'm sorry you have felt this way," said Duane with Carol echoing his sentiments. "I wish you had told us about this sooner. I can see how your mother and I may have neglected you in our need to care for Davy. I guess we just assumed that you could take care of yourself, and that was wrong. Unfortunately, we have no choice when it comes to Davy. He can't take care of himself, and we will always have to be there for him. However, as your dad I will try to make more time for us to do some things together. I realize

my work often gets in the way with this. It's too bad there isn't another good mechanic in town who can take some of the pressure off me."

"Thanks for giving me a clearer picture of what has been happening all these years," said Trent. "That in itself means a lot. You don't need to worry about spending that much time with me. I'm going to be very busy getting ready to go to college this fall and spending as much time as I can with Sally before I leave here. She was the one who told me I should talk with you, and I'm very glad I took her advice."

The next time Trent met up with Sally, he told her how he had talked to Duane, and things were much better since they had gotten everything out in the open. However, he didn't say that he was still embarrassed at having Davy as a brother and never expected that to change.

"Time will tell if I'm accepted into the NFL," Trent told Sally. "I plan to study mechanical engineering so I will have a good job just in case I don't make it. It would be great if you could join me in LA and start your cosmetology business there. I think there will be a lot more opportunities for us in a larger area. We can get married and raise a family there if that's what you want."

"You know that's what I want," said Sally.

They parted not knowing that things might well

change. No one ever knows what the future might hold, and it can change in a heartbeat, and lives can never be the same again.

Duane made good on his promise to spend more time with Trent. Fortunately, he was able to hire another good mechanic to work with him which gave him the free time he had always wanted. Carol appreciated this, too. She and Duane were finally able to spend more time together and put back some of the romance that had been sorely lacking in their marriage. Trent sensed less tension between his parents which made him far more at ease. Duane and Carol took a trip to Sacramento where they visited the Old Town area, spending a couple of nights there and getting to know each other better. They were able to leave Davy with a good friend of theirs in the meantime. Things definitely were looking up in the Harding household.

Around the middle of the summer Sally told Trent that her parents were going away for a weekend and said they could have the place to themselves. Trent was somewhat surprised that Sally would want him to come there.

"Are you sure you are ok with this?" he asked. "Absolutely," said Sally.

So that weekend Trent went prepared to spend the night there just in case Sally wanted him to. He wasn't sure what would happen, but he knew it might be something totally unexpected. Sally greeted him at the door, and he felt a stirring in his loins as soon as he saw her. Sally was wearing a black satin negligee which contrasted with her clear pale skin. Trent had never seen her look more beautiful, and he was filled with desire. With trembling hands, he pulled off the gown, and Sally stood naked before him. He felt his member harden and quickly stripped off his clothing to reveal his well-toned body and firm abs. They stood caressing each other. Trent moved his hands over Sally's small breasts which were like two porcelain orbs, then made his way down her hips while kissing her lips and inserting his tongue into her mouth. He then kissed and fondled her breasts, moving further down to kiss her pubic hair. Sally did the same with him. Suddenly he was lying on the bed on top of her, his whole body convulsing with desire. Sally raised her hips, moaning and panting, and all at once he was inside her, his member moving back and forth, until he finally reached climax. He knew it was her first time as it was his and hoped she had found it pleasurable. Turning on his back, he lay there with the sweat running off him.

"Did it hurt? I never wanted to hurt you."

"Just a little at first, but then it was wonderful," replied Sally. "There is blood on the mattress!" she gasped.

"That's because I broke your cherry and why you felt some pain at first."

They lay there until they fell asleep in each other's arms, knowing how much they loved each

18

other. What could ever change that? Naturally Sally never told her parents.

The Fourth of July arrived signaling the onset of summer. As usual there were flags hung outside homes, and there was the usual big parade on Main Street with the Rhodes High marching band and a number of decorated floats. The citizens of Rhodes always made a show of being very patriotic. They tended to shun those who weren't. Trent and Sally always enjoyed seeing the parade, and this year was no exception. That night there was a big BBQ in the park where everyone feasted on hot dogs, hamburgers, and apple pie along with other picnic style treats supplied by some local restaurants. Then as darkness fell, there was a display of fireworks with everyone cheering the grand finale. It was a perfect end to the holiday.

A couple of weeks later came the annual county fair. Trent and Sally went, feasting on cotton candy and corn dogs.

"There's nothing like fair food, even though it's not good for you," said Trent.

"I totally agree," said Sally. "Well, it only comes once a year so so we can afford to indulge."

After eating their fill, they went over to the carnival area and took rides on both the Ferris wheel and the Tilt-a -Whirl. Sally hated to go on any rides that turned one upside down, so they crossed those off the list. As usual Trent won a large stuffed animal to give to Sally after winning one of the games in the carnival area. They also ventured over to the Fine Arts building and later on to see the livestock. Sally always enjoyed seeing the rabbits and chickens. One of the pigs had just given birth to ten piglets, and the sow was busy suckling them. They both took a look at the cows, horses and sheep. They stayed until it was getting dark making the most of a wonderful day at the fair. Their only regret was that summer was soon coming to a close.

A few weeks later Trent got an early morning

call from Sally, and she sounded stressed. She asked him to meet her at the park as soon as possible as she needed to talk to him. Trent threw on some clothes and headed straight over there. He found Sally seated on a bench looking very pale and drawn. Trent was immediately concerned that something unforeseen must have happened.

"What is it? I can see you are upset. Has something happened?" "I'm pregnant," said Sally.

"Are you sure?" asked Trent, dumbfounded by what he had just heard.

"I'm sure. I took a test and it was positive. I never thought this could happen. After all it was our first time, but I should have known better. This is all my fault as I was the one who instigated this. God is punishing me for committing sin."

"God is not punishing you. I should have taken precautions and worn a condom. If anyone is to blame it's me."

"I guess we both share the blame," said Sally. "What do you want to do?" asked Trent.

"There is no way I'm keeping it. My parents can never know. They would disown me, and I couldn't bear to have that happen. You have to understand. I want to get an abortion as soon as possible."

"I understand. There is no way I am ready to be a father either. I have always wanted kids, but now is not the time. I'm about to head off to college and have my whole future planned out. We can go to Sacramento and find a clinic there. We can easily make it up and back in one day, and no one will be the wiser. We can say we want to have one final fling this summer, visit the Old Town area and have dinner there."

"That sounds like the best idea possible," said Sally. "Thank you for supporting me in this."

"I love you Sally, so how could I do otherwise?"

When Trent mentioned these plans to his

parents, Duane offered to lend them his car so they wouldn't have to take a bus. His parents

bought the idea that this was a last pleasure trip before Trent headed to UCLA, and they felt he deserved it after all he had accomplished. That didn't keep Trent from being overwhelmed by guilt. He didn't see how he could ever forgive himself not only for making Sally pregnant but for lying to his parents. What was until now the best summer of his life was turning out to be the worst one.

That night Trent lay awake for most of the night as did Sally. She was also consumed by guilt and wondered if her life would ever be the same. She had always been against abortion, and here she was about to have one. She feared she would never enter heaven, and God would sentence her to eternal punishment. She knew about the fires in hell from reading the Bible, and the thought of being eternally burning in hell was unimaginable. She was afraid of going to sleep lest she have nightmares. Her world had suddenly been turned upside down, and there seemed no way to ever right it again.

Trent and Sally remained mostly silent on the way to Sacramento the next day. They got off to an early start so they could be sure and have time to look up a clinic there that performed abortions. Trent had already researched out one the day before and had written down the address. Once they arrived there, they noticed several people picketing outside holding up anti-abortion signs. That made Sally feel all the more guilty. Once they entered, Sally was taken into a room to meet with a doctor who asked her if this is what she really wanted to do. He said the clinic offered counseling services and asked if she would like to speak with someone. He said he did not approve of abortion on demand solely for the purpose of getting rid of a fetus. Would she prefer having the baby and then giving it up for adoption? However, Sally remained adamant that she wanted an abortion, and there was no

24

talking her out of it. She underwent some tests beforehand to see how far along she was with the pregnancy which was estimated to be about six weeks. The actual procedure only took a few minutes, and afterwards Sally was given some medication to help with any pain. However, the only pain she felt was psychological.

When she rejoined Trent in the waiting room, she didn't want to discuss anything that had happened; she just wanted to start back home. Neither of them had any appetite for dinner even though they hadn't eaten anything since early morning. They remained in their own worlds on the drive back.

"How was the trip?" asked Duane. He and Carol both wanted to hear all about it, but Trent begged off saying he was feeling tired from having been on the go all day and thought he needed a good night's rest. He went upstairs, and again he lay awake for a long time before finally falling into a restless sleep.

Sally also lay awake until she finally drifted off only to have a nightmare about entering the gates of hell.

Several days after their trip to Sacramento, Trent and Sally met once more in the park. It was a painful meeting for both of them, as they spent time discussing how they could best move forward.

"I hope this is not the end for us," said Trent. I love you with all my heart. I hope you feel the same way."

"I do love you, Trent," said Sally. "But I just need time to myself for a while to think things over and hopefully come to terms with all this. I hope you will understand and be patient with me. You will be heading off to college soon which will give us some time apart, and that will be good for both of us. I promise that I will email you regularly and keep in touch."

"That will be great, and, yes, I will try to be patient, because I love so much," Trent replied.

But in the end Sally never kept her promise. She never emailed Trent, and she never stayed in touch with him. Trent made every effort to contact her, but he finally had to face the fact that perhaps he had lost her forever which grieved him deeply.

When Trent's parents asked why he was not seeing Sally, he just lied saying they both needed some time apart to adjust to his leaving for college soon. Sally said the same to Mitch and Linda adding that she needed to focus on studying cosmetology. She tried to put on the best front as possible, although it took all her will power to do so. She would never get over the guilt of having the abortion.

Trent knew he needed to start getting ready for UCLA even though his heart was not in it as it had been. Until this happened, he had been so excited about the prospect of going to college, playing football, and studying mechanical engineering. He just prayed that things would change for the better once he got there.

A couple of weeks later he, his parents and Davy took off for UCLA. They decided to drive there so they could see the country. Besides both Duane and Carol hated flying. Davy was excited and bounced up and down in his seat until Trent shouted at him to stop. Davy burst into tears, and Duane told him to apologize.

"You need to put a lid on it son," said Duane. "Sorry," said Trent.

"Tell Davy you are sorry, not to me."

"Hey bro, don't mind what I said. It's ok, just stop crying." Davy wiped away his tears and smiled at Trent. He looked up to his older brother and always had despite Trent's rejection of him. He didn't have the capacity to understand otherwise.

They stayed overnight in a motel and finally reached LA late the next day. It was warm and sunny but not nearly as hot as in Rhodes. Trent was assigned a dorm room with another fellow named Joe Forrester. Joe was also there on a football scholarship so they would have that in common. However, Joe was majoring in biology and planned to be a marine biologist as a backup to being drafted into the NFL or not. Joe said he came from San Jose. He was a bit shorter than Trent with a stockier build. His face was somewhat pock marked by acne scars, and he was nowhere near as handsome as Trent. Trent could immediately see that Joe was really neat about his side of the room, so he would have to shape up and stop being careless like he was in the habit of being at home. He rarely hung up his clothes and tended to leave wet towels on the bathroom floor which irritated Carol no end. That wasn't going to go over well with Joe.

Later that day Trent and his family were given a tour of the campus, and Trent picked up the schedule of his classes. As always, he was ashamed of being seen with Davy, but there was nothing he could do about it. He tended to walk a bit ahead so he wouldn't feel as self-conscious.

That night the four of them had one final dinner together at an Italian restaurant not far from campus. His parents and Davy would start for home early the next morning, so they parted company there. Carol got a bit teary as she knew she was going to miss Trent. Duane shook his hand and wished him well.

"You be sure to write or email as often as possible,"said Carol. "I will," replied Trent.

So that was it. He was on his own to either sink or swim. He didn't feel the confidence he once had back at graduation. He just hoped it would return in time so he could be as successful here as he had been all through high school.

Classes started that following Monday, and Trent's first one was English. It had never been his favorite subject as he preferred math instead, but he always did well in any class.

30

Turns out what worked the best at restoring his confidence was playing football. He loved being on the team and always showed up for practice. Coach Sanders said he showed a lot of promise and could well see him being drafted into the NFL. That caused Trent to work even harder. He was also acing all of his classes, even English. Learning had always come easily to Trent, and he didn't have to study all that much to do well. He had also signed up to be a math tutor a couple of hours on the weekends when he was free to do that. He and Joe were becoming good friends both on the football field and elsewhere. They enjoyed spending time together and often went off campus to have a burger when the dorm food did not appeal to them. Joe was also being considered for the NFL. He was not quite the outstanding student that Trent was, but he did well enough to deserve his scholarship. Things might have continued to go well for the remainder of the semester if something totally unexpected hadn't happened.

One morning several weeks later Trent woke up feeling like he was suddenly in a very dark place. Overnight a black cloud had descended over him, and he had no idea what was wrong. All he knew is that he had no desire to get up and go to his early morning class, nor go to football practice in the afternoon. What could have happened? Why did he feel this way? He could think of no plausible explanation. It seemed as if his mind had gone numb, and that scared him. He had never felt so frightened in his entire life. How could something like this have happened just overnight? Joe had already left for his early class, and Trent saw his was now long over. He had awakened mid-morning, and his class started at 8:00. He struggled to get up and go to the bathroom, but then headed right back to bed, pulling the covers over his head to block out the light. It was a beautiful sunny day, but Trent saw only darkness as he crawled into a fetal position and fell back to sleep, only to have strange dark dreams.

Joe returned late in the afternoon and was surprised to find Trent still in bed.

"Hey dude, what wrong? Are you sick"? You weren't at football practice today, and Coach Sanders was wondering where you were. I told him I would find out and let him know as we were roommates. I assume you didn't make it to your classes today either. What should I tell coach?"

"Don't tell him anything. It's none of his business and none of yours either. I didn't feel like showing up for practice or classes either. In fact, I no longer want to be in this room or on this campus"

"What are you saying, man? You love being here playing football. We both do. We make a great team. We were just saying that last night. We both have a good chance at making the NFL. Why would want to throw that all away?"

"Things can change."

"They don't change that quickly, not just overnight. You need to level with me. I don't buy this for one minute."

"That's your problem. I'd appreciate it if you just left me alone." Joe knew something terrible must have happened; he just didn't know what. Tomorrow he would talk to Coach Sanders, and maybe they could try to figure out what to do. Joe decided to work in the library instead of staying in the room, because he knew he was not welcome there. He left feeling very uneasy and totally at a loss as to how he should handle things. Trent had become a good friend, and he wanted to stick by him in any way he could.

Several days later Trent was called into the freshman dean's office. Coach Sanders was also there. The dean got straight to the point.

"Trent, I see you have been cutting classes and also football practice. I need to know what's going on. You have had perfect attendance both in class and on the field ever since you got here. Coach Sanders said you are on track for being drafted into the NFL.

Your roommate, Joe Forrester, has told us you no longer want to be here. Again, I really need to know what's going on.

Joe said you were fine until one morning recently when everything seemed to change overnight. There has to be a reason for this, and I would like to know what it is."

"I don't have to have a reason. It's just the way it is. I'm telling you I want to leave here and the sooner the better."

"I took the liberty of phoning your parents, and they said you hadn't told them anything about this. They sounded as baffled as we are," said the dean. "They don't want you to leave here until we get to the bottom of this. We have a good counseling service here on campus, and I would like you to see one of our counselors immediately."

35

"I'm not crazy," retorted Trent. "I don't need to see a shrink."

"I'm not saying you are crazy. It just means we think you need help with whatever has caused this abrupt change. Your parents agree and don't want you to come home until you have given this a try." "Suit yourself, but you will, be wasting both your time and mine"

"We'll see about that."

The meeting left both the dean and Coach Sanders very disturbed. Trent had been such a gifted student and an outstanding football player. Why on earth would he want to throw this all away? What possibly could have happened so suddenly? It simply didn't make sense. His roommate Joe was equally concerned. He prayed that Trent would decide to see a counselor and get the help that he needed. He couldn't imagine Trent leaving UCLA when he had loved being there and playing football. Someone needed to get to the bottom of this mystery and the sooner the better.

What was also a mystery was why Trent seemed to want to act upon this so quickly without putting more thought into it which is what a normal person would do. However, this just showed that Trent was not normal and obviously was very ill indeed.

Trent did meet with a counselor, but just as he predicted, nothing was resolved. Trent refused to reveal anything. The counselor did say that she thought Trent was suffering from an onslaught of depression. She had seen other cases where this could come on very quickly, especially in someone Trent's age. Unfortunately, Duane refused to agree with this. He saw mental illness as a sign of weakness. No son of his could be labeled mentally ill. In time he would come to regret this.

So, Trent was allowed to leave the university. He never said goodbye to Joe which grieved Joe deeply. He wished he could have found some way to help his friend. He had done all he could, but it was not enough. He just hoped that Trent would recover from what seemed to be a terrible illness. Back home in Rhodes, Trent never contacted Sally, as he was too ashamed to do so. Plus, he felt that since she had never stayed in touch with him as she had promised, she would not want to see him anyway. He spent his days in bed or wandering the streets aimlessly. He stopped showering and refused to change clothes. His thick brown hair became matted, and there were dark circles under his eyes. He barely recognized himself in the mirror. He had always taken such pride in his appearance. The person looking back at him was a stranger. He had also lost a significant amount of weight. Lack of exercise had caused his once well-toned body to sag. He had no appetite and ate next to nothing despite Carol pleading with him to eat more. She begged Duane to do something, but her entreaties fell on deaf ears.

"He'll snap out of it," said Duane. "Just give him time." However, Carol was beginning to fear for Trent's life. She just couldn't understand why Duane wanted to stand by and do nothing. She lay awake nights thinking about this and how she would never forgive herself if anything happened to Trent.

Eventually Trent started medicating himself with alcohol. Since his parents did not keep any alcohol at home, Trent managed to persuade a friend to keep him supplied. The friend's parents drank and thought nothing of their son giving alcohol to Trent. In fact, they had always thought of Duane and Carol as a pair of goody-two-shoes, so in a way this was getting back at them. Trent hid the beer cans in a large suitcase in his closet. He drank late at night hoping it would help him fall asleep, but sleep tended to allude him, and nights were as dark as the days.

Late one night unbeknownst to his parents, Trent took his father's car and went out joy riding.

He took along a six-pack of beer and consumed several cans while driving. He never saw the car pull out in front of him that had the green light in its direction. He slammed into the passenger's side, but by then he was so intoxicated that he had no idea what happened. Bystanders phoned 911, and soon several police cars and an ambulance were on the scene. The driver of the other car was a young woman who appeared to be seriously injured. After she was taken out of her car, it was determined that she should be air-lifted by helicopter to Sacramento since Rhodes didn't have the proper facilities to treat her there.

When Trent was pulled from the car, he was so drunk he could barely stand let alone walk in a straight line. The police found open beer cans in his car and determined there and then that both cars were totaled. Several bystanders recognized Trent and couldn't believe he was the same person. His appearance was so altered that they had to take a second look to realize it was him. They knew he was supposed to be at UCLA, so what was he doing back here, and why was he intoxicated? Trent was taken to the county jail where he spent the night trying to sober up. The police contacted his parents and told them they could pick him up the next morning, but he was guilty of some very serious charges, including underage drinking.

When Duane and Carol went to the jail around 8:00 the next morning, they were stunned to see how bad Trent looked. His face and forehead were bruised from being thrown against the dashboard. He had not been wearing a seat belt, so it was a wonder that he had not been thrown into the windshield. His face was ashen, and he remained totally silent. He had been up all night, vomiting, and he was totally drained. His parents thought it best not to question him about what happened or why he had been drinking. They only knew he needed help. It finally was a wake-up call for

Duane. He never faced that fact as he should have that Trent was indeed mentally ill.

Once they got home, Duane helped Trent take a much overdue bath. Soaking in the warm tub water seemed to relax him, and some color started returning to his face. Duane gently washed his hair, then helped him out and gave him a pair of warm pajamas, after which he helped him into bed. Sleep was what he needed now, and for the first time in many days Trent did not have any nightmares.

Several days later Trent went before a judge who decided that because he had no prior felonies and had done so well in the past, he required him to do a year of community service instead of spending time in jail. He also said that Trent must see a doctor immediately and get on the proper medication to help with his depression. Trent was more than willing to agree to all of this as he knew that he needed help. The depression was what caused him to drop out of UCLA and give up everything he had worked so hard to achieve. Duane in turn realized that he had been wrong in believing that mental illness was a weakness and should be kept hidden away. He blamed himself for what happened, because if he had forced Trent to take medication, maybe none of this would have happened.

The judge assigned Trent to perform his community service at a group home for young men with severe behavior problems located in the San Jose area. For someone who had grown up and spent almost all of his life in Rhodes, this would be a radical change. Right before he was due to leave, he found out that the family of the injured woman had decided not to sue. Fortunately, she was recovering well and would be released from the hospital soon. When her family learned about what an exemplary life Trent had led in the past and that he was being treated for depression, they wanted to give him a second chance.

Sally heard what happened to Trent, but she chose not to contact him. She decided they should continue to go their separate ways. He was no longer the same person anymore that she once knew.

Shortly before he was to leave for San Jose, Trent told Duane that he wanted to contact the freshman dean and his coach at UCLA and apologize to them for his behavior there. After returning home, he realized he was seriously mentally ill. He had undergone therapy and had started taking medication. Unfortunately, right after returning home, he had gotten into serious trouble and was having to do a year of community service. Consequently, he never would be returning to UCLA, as his future would be taking a different path. He appreciated all they had tried to do for him. He also wanted to let his former roommate, Joe Forester, know how much he valued his friendship and how Joe had tried to help him. He hoped Joe would make it into the NFL. Coach Sanders said he was certain this would happen. Joe was very relieved to hear this, and he made sure to contact Trent to wish him the very best. He told Trent he would always consider him to be his friend. Joe did end up making it into the NFL, and Trent made it a point to congratulate him.

Trent and his parents then drove to San Jose where Trent was about to learn that his life would be changed forever

A Search for Purpose

PART 2

A Search for Purpose

Joby

Unfortunately, some people are born with terrible deformities. They never know what it is like to walk down a street without having people stare at them, point fingers at them or call them names. Mothers tell their children to look away and not stare, but they end up staring themselves. People tend to fear what they don't understand, and this can be played out in various ways Some react with pity, others with derision. They forget that these unfortunate souls are not freaks on the inside.

Early one morning in 1976, an Episcopal priest at a church just outside of Roseville, California, found a male infant lying next to the church's front door.

Close examination showed that the infant was just recently born, as part of the umbilical cord was still attached. He was wrapped naked inside a urine-soaked blanket with a note attached to it which read, "My name is Job." Maybe the mother was familiar with the Old Testament book of Job in which the major theme is suffering. The name certainly seemed appropriate. The priest had never seen anything so strange. The infant's nose bridge was missing making his upturned nostrils resembled a snout. Meanwhile the lower part of his face was somewhat elongated, dipping lower than it should have below the nostrils making it resemble a canine's muzzle. The last two fingers on each hand were missing, and both the wrists and ankles were turned slightly inward. The priest immediately called for an ambulance which took Job to the nearest hospital. There the rest of the umbilical cord was removed, and he was diapered and giving fresh clothing. He was obviously hungry, so one of the nurses gave him some sugar water and later a bottle of milk which he downed in short order. Fearing people might be upset at seeing him in the hospital nursery, he was placed in a bassinet in a separate room.

Despite conducting an extensive search and having Job's picture in local papers, the mother was never found, so eventually he was placed in the foster care system. They never expected anyone to foster him, but an older couple named Don and Louise Emery who had no children saw Job's picture and wanted to take him. They were devout Christians who felt that God never makes mistakes, and every child has a purpose.

The next ten years were the best that Job would ever spend. The Emerys were devoted to him and saw to it that he had the best life possible. They took him to their church where he was welcomed into the congregation and had him baptized there.

However, one sunny day in late fall, Job's life was forever changed. The three of them were on a short trip when they met with a terrible accident.

Another car crossed over into their lane and hit

them head on. Both Don and Louise died at the scene, but somehow Job had survived uninjured. He was riding strapped into the back seat, and maybe this shielded him from the brunt of the impact.

Job was devastated about losing this wonderful couple. They had always treated him like their son, and he didn't know how he could survive without them. He cried himself to sleep for days, not knowing what would become of him and not wanting to go on living.

Once again Job was placed in the foster care system, and after he turned twelve a couple named Rick and Arlene Webster finally came forth to foster him. If the foster care system had not been so understaffed and overworked, they would never have placed Job with this couple. They failed to investigate Rick's background or they would have seen that he had once been arrested for child abuse. Rick was a heavyset burly man, and his wife feared him. He had abused her in the past as well and kept her under a tight rein. They lived in a rundown place near San Jose where the front yard was cluttered with everything imaginable. Despite neighbors' complaints, nothing was ever done. Truth be known, Rick's neighbors feared him as well. They knew he kept guns and had a bad temper.

Once Job arrived there, his nightmare began. Rick locked him in the basement, and immediately the abuse began. He taped Job's mouth shut so no one could hear him scream. He threw him face down on the cement floor and proceeded to rape him. Job felt as if a hot poker had entered his anus, and the pain was unspeakable, made even more terrible as Job had not yet reached puberty.

"Like that you little freak?" snarled Rick. "Get used to it because, there will be a lot more to come."

Rick made good on his word. He continued to rape Job on a daily basis. Sometimes he used other objects like a broom handle or a screwdriver. Every

53

time there was bleeding and terrible pain. Rick also performed other unspeakable acts. He burned Job with cigarettes and a hot knife he had held over a stove burner. He poured scalding water over his hands leaving large blisters. He made Job drink his urine and eat his feces which caused Job to vomit. He then smeared the vomit back on Job's face which only made him vomit more. He beat him unmercifully using an electrical cord across Job's back and buttocks which cut into the skin and would leave him forever scarred. Other times he hit Job's backside with a heavy paddle leaving him black and blue on top of the cuts which were already there. It was so painful that he could barely sit down. He delighted in dragging Job across the room by his hair or yanking onto it to draw him up into a sitting position. He fed him nothing but moldy bread and spoiled food which constantly made him sick and feverish. Another time Rick used a pair of rusty pliers to take out some of Job's teeth which caused him even more pain as his mouth became infected, and he could hardly chew. Eventually Job retreated into himself, and Rick no longer had to tape his mouth shut, as he became completely mute. He never uttered another word. He was locked into silence and felt as if his soul had left him. This made Rick even more angry, and the abuse became even worse.

Job might well have died, if one day Rick had not left the house forgetting to lock the basement door. Arlene saw this as an opportunity for them both to escape. She found Job lying naked on the floor looking like no more than a skeleton and covered with bruises from head to foot. Wrapping him in a blanket, she could easily carry him upstairs where they fled to a neighbor's house. The neighbor was so shocked at seeing Job that she wondered for a moment if he was human. Once she regained her composure, she immediately phoned the police. When Rick arrived back home, two police cars were there waiting for him. They surrounded his car so he could not escape and took him into custody where he was booked into the county jail and held without bail. He was sentenced to 20 years in prison at the state penitentiary in Folsom, and the judge doubted if he would ever be paroled. He offered no remorse and sneered at the judge the whole time he was in the courtroom. The judge wished he could have sentenced Rick to life in prison, but this was the most he could do. His wife Arlene was declared innocent, as she was also a victim. She moved to Oregon to live with a sister who never suspected the hellish life Arlene had led. For the first time in many years Arlene found some peace.

The judge need not have worried, because a few months later Rick was stabbed to death by another inmate while he was in the prison courtyard for an hour's daily exercise. If it had not been done by this inmate, another probably would have done so, as Rick had made a lot of enemies due to his conviction for terrible child abuse.

Unfortunately, the peace that Arlene felt was not true for Job. When he arrived at the hospital, he stood at five foot two inches but weighed barely 60 pounds, having once weighed twice that. For a while he had to be tube fed as his digestive system had shut down, and he could barely swallow. He had surgery to remove adhesions which were in his anal area due to the trauma he had suffered during Rick's assaults. Although he would never be quite the same, he found it much easier to go to the bathroom. There was no more bleeding, and the pain stopped. After a while the feeding tube was removed, and Job started taking small amounts of soft food. He found it hard to chew because his teeth were full of cavities, and he would need extensive dental work done in the future. Antibiotics helped clear up the infection in the areas where Rick had removed several teeth. Fortunately, he was up on all of his vaccinations thanks to his time with the Emerys, or he probably would have gotten tetanus. An attractive young nurse named

Julie tried to coax him to eat, often spoon feeding him. One day Job said, "It hurts." They were the first words he had uttered in almost two years.

"Where does it hurt, honey?"

Job placed his hand over his heart saying, "Hurts here."

Tears welled up in Julie's eyes as she knew what he meant. He was telling her he was heart sick.

Regaining his speech was a major accomplishment for Job. He gradually started gaining weight, and his color improved. However, he still had a long way to go. Many nights he awoke screaming from having terrible nightmares. Julie would rush in, take him in her arms and try to soothe him back to sleep. The doctors agreed that he should remain in the hospital free of charge for the time being, after which they planned to send him to a rehab center where he would remain indefinitely.

They wanted him to begin having therapy for

post-traumatic-stress disorder brought on by the abuse. At first Job just sat there silently, but after a while he gradually started opening up. He talked about what his life was like during the years he was living with the Emerys. Finally, he was able to shed tears, and his body was wracked by sobs. It was a major breakthrough, and from then on, he began the long road to recovery. What helped even further was knowing that Rick had been killed in prison, and he would no longer have to fear ever seeing him again. Over the next few years, with proper diet and care, Job grew another six inches to reach his final height of five feet eight inches.

The therapist never expected Job to fully recover or that one day Job would prove him wrong. He just wanted him to be able to function again.

Once he was finally released from the rehab center, the therapist recommended that Job be placed in a group home in San Jose with other young men who had undergone similar problems, although to a far lesser degree. By then Job was 19 years old. In retrospect this did not prove to be the best thing for him at first, but later on it did. It was there that Job would meet someone who would change his life.

PART 3

A Search for Purpose

Trent and Joby

Once Duane and Carol arrived in San Jose, leaving Davy at home with a friend, they drove directly to the group home where Trent would be spending the next year. He was filled with anxiety about what would happen there. The home was located in a residential area with other similar homes, although it was larger. Five young men were living there, and once Job arrived there were six. The head of the home greeted them at the door and immediately invited them in. He introduced himself as Dean Lockwood, and he probably was around 40 years old. He had a short beard and dark brown hair which was showing some streaks of gray. He looked like the athletic type.

"How was your flight? I trust you didn't have any trouble finding the place. You must be Trent," he said. "Glad to have you with us. I do have to say I know why you are here, and I will keep a close

63

watch on you at all times. You will be mentoring one of our newest residents named Job. It will not be an easy case as you will see, but I feel you can do the job. We will be having a house meeting shortly, so let me get you settled in and show you your room. You can unpack later."

With that Trent said goodbye to his parents. He refrained from confessing how much he was going to miss them. He felt an ache in the back of his throat and had to fight to hold back the tears.

Just as Trent was about to head upstairs to his room, he heard a commotion. Someone was calling Dean to hurry outside for some reason. Trent ran back downstairs just as Dean was heading out the front door. There he saw the reason for the problem. Backed up against the garage door was the strangest- looking person Trent had ever seen. Tears were streaming down his face which he was trying to cover with his hands. Trent saw that he was missing two fingers on each of them, and both

64

wrists were bent inward as well as both his ankles which caused him to move from side to side as he walked. A group of younger neighborhood boys were taunting him.

"Hey pig face, oink, oink," one of them shouted. "Dog face," screamed another.

"Hey freak, Look at the freak crying. Let's see you cry freak."

"That's enough," said Dean in a loud voice which caused the kids to scatter.

"It's ok, Job. What are you doing out here anyway?"

"They were bullying me in there and I just wanted to escape," said Job in a surprisingly deep voice which was choked with sobs.

Dean put his arm around Job and drew him close. It was clear that he felt deeply sorry for him. After the initial shock at seeing Job, Trent felt a sense of pity and decided that he would make it his mission to help this poor soul the best way he could.

The group meeting was held shortly thereafter. Trent made it a point to sit next to Job, but Job looked down and remained silent.

"I'm really disappointed in you all," said Dean. "There is no excuse

for bullying anyone. We are here to help each other and get our behavior under control. You know very clearly why you are here. I want each of

you eventually to be able to live independently, but that's not going to happen if things don't start to change. Trent is here doing community service for something he has done in the past. He also needs to be accepted by you. Right now, I want you to go to your rooms and remain there until dinner. Think about this, and make it a point that what happened here today doesn't happen again."

As Dean expected things did improve a bit but not nearly as much as he wanted them to. When the group saw that Trent was leaning towards having sympathy for Job, they started ostracizing him as well. One afternoon something very disturbing happened. One member of the group found Dean's favorite cap that he always like to wear, and the others decided it would be fun to throw it on the roof and challenge Trent to retrieve it.

"See if you can get it down. We'll say you put it up there, and it will be your word against ours. Let's see how brave you are."

Trent had always been afraid of heights. It was something Duane had taunted him about, but this time he felt he had no choice. He would have to make the effort. He got a ladder from the garage and proceeded to climb up to the roof, all the while being terrified to look down. Once there, he very gingerly stepped onto the roof. However, just as he was about to take hold of the cap, he suddenly lost his footing and fell backwards. No doubt he would have been seriously injured or killed if the bottom

67

of his pant leg hadn't been caught on a large nail leaving him dangling upside down. Job heard his screams and came outside to see what was happening. As soon as Trent saw him, he cried out, "Joby help me! Go get Dean!"

Dean came running out as soon as Job went inside to find him. He immediately was aware of the gravity of the situation and his need to calm Trent down.

"Don't move. I'm coming up. You will be ok."

Trent was sobbing in fear. He had never felt so scared in his life, and he thought for sure he was about to die. Job looked up at him with his hands pressed over his heart. Dean quickly climbed the ladder which was next to where Trent was dangling. He then went down a few rungs until he could grab Trent under his shoulders. Only by some miracle was he able to tear the nail from Trent's pant leg and pull Trent next to him, helping him climb onto the ladder in front of him. When they were finally able to reach the ground, Trent grabbed a hold of Dean and hugged him. He had never been so grateful to anyone in his entire life. He also went over to Job and thanked him for getting Dean to come out so quickly.

"You also saved my life."

Job looked down and said shyly, "I like Joby better."

So, from then on Job became known as Joby. The five other housemates ended up confessing that they were to blame for this and apologized to Trent. Trent was more than happy to accept their apology knowing that they had learned from this, and it would never happen again. Dean went back up on the roof and retrieved his cap. He decided that the group had learned a valuable lesson from this and decided further punishment was not necessary.

From then on things changed. The group stopped bullying Joby, and made sure the neighborhood kids never did so anymore either.

Joby started feeling much better about himself. Things finally seemed to be turning around for him at the group home.

One day Trent found Joby looking rather downcast and asked him what was the matter. Joby got rather teary-eyed and said, "I know I shouldn't say this, but I envy you Trent. You are handsome and will get married someday, but no one will ever want me. I will never get married. I will never have kids. My heart aches for that."

"You don't know that, Joby. No one can ever be sure of whatever the future holds. As the saying goes, God moves in mysterious ways. We don't know what God has in store for us. We just have to have faith." "That's easier said than done for me," said Joby.

"I'm sure it is," replied Trent. "But whatever happens, I will I will always be your friend."

Joby threw his arms around Trent and tearfully hugged him. "You are my best friend in the whole world."

"And you are mine," said Trent.

Christmas was just around the corner, and everyone was starting to make plans for the holidays. The other residents of the group home had families they could go home to, and they were more than welcome to do so now that they had gotten their behavior much better under control. Only Joby had no family and would be the only one remaining behind along with Dean. It made him very sad indeed until one day shortly before Christmas Trent changed everything.

"I want you to come home with me for Christmas," said Trent. Joby couldn't believe his ears. "Really, are you sure?" "Absolutely. My parents, and my brother Davy will be arriving here tomorrow to take us all back to Rhodes. Trust me it's not much of a town, but it will be great to have you there. I think you should start packing as knowing my parents, they will want to get an early

71

start back there before the traffic gets too bad."

"OK!" He threw his arms around Trent and hugged him. "You are the best friend I could ever want, "said Joby, shedding tears.

"Do your parents know what I what I look like?" he asked, once he had regained his composure.

"Yes, they do. I sent them a picture of the two of us together. A picture is worth a thousand words as they say."

The Hardings made the trip to San Jose which took most of the day. Joby knew that Davy had Down's syndrome, and Trent had avoided talking about him in the past. He suspected that Trent might be ashamed of Davy which he felt was unusual considering how much he had accepted him. When Duane, Carol and Davy exited the car, Davy tore right over and threw his arms around Joby.

"Do you want to be my friend?" Davy asked,

struggling to make his words understandable.

"You bet I do," replied Joby, giving Davy a good squeeze in return. Trent immediately realized that this was the way he should have treated Davy all along. Davy was nothing to be ashamed of. He was the same as Joby, both dealing with disabilities over which they had no control. They were two young men who could well relate to one another.

On the trip back to Rhodes, Joby chose to sit next to Davy. They played some simple games together, one being, "I Spy." Whenever they spotted some cows grazing in pastures along the freeway, they competed with each other on who could say, "I spy" the first. Davy delighted in playing this, and Joby made sure he won most of the time. Trent knew that this was what he should have been doing himself, and he would always regret not having done so.

They arrived in Rhodes by late afternoon, and decided to stop at McDonalds which was Davy's favorite place. He loved getting hamburgers and French fries there and maybe a hot fudge sundae if he was lucky. They all decided to go inside to eat. Once again Joby sat beside Davy in a booth and wiped his face as Davy was not the neatest eater. Duane and Carol were very touched by this and so was Trent.

The house was well-decorated for Christmas inside and out. Ornaments hung from the branches of a live Christmas tree which gave off a wonderful smell of pine. Carol didn't like artificial trees as there was no pine aroma to them. There were some brightly colored packages under the tree.

A nativity set was on display on a nearby table and various other decorations throughout the house. There was a large wreath hanging on the front door along with several other outdoor decorations. The entire place looked very festive. Davy had always loved Christmas and still believed in Santa Claus even though he was now 17. Consequently, his parents never put his gifts out until Christmas morning, telling him that Santa was coming just for him. Carol wrote down what he wanted for Christmas and made sure these things were under the tree waiting for him on Christmas morning. Davy always wanted to leave cookies there for Santa on Christmas Eve.

As usual, Davy was up at the crack of dawn waking up everyone else in his eagerness to see what Santa had left him. Carol made sure the cookies were removed so Davy would think that Santa had taken them. His gifts were set apart to make Davy think that Santa had only left special gifts for him. Joby sat on the floor next to Davy helping him as he fumbled trying to open the packages. He squealed in delight when he discovered that Santa had brought him everything on his list.

Duane and Carol gave Joby a book about the history of Rhodes when Trent told them he enjoyed reading books, especially ones about history. Trent gave him colorful cap, and Davy gave him a finger painting he had done in his special education class. This time Joby couldn't hold back the tears and said he was sorry he hadn't given any presents in return.

"You had no idea you were coming here so you have nothing to be sorry about," said Trent. "Besides, just having you here is gift enough."

Duane and Carol were in complete agreement. They sat down to a wonderful breakfast of scrambled eggs, bacon, biscuits with sausage gravy and fresh fruit. Later that afternoon they feasted on turkey, stuffing, sweet potato casserole, cranberry sauce, green beans with bacon and onion and mince pie for dessert. Joby had never seen so much food in his entire life and ate until he felt over stuffed. He could well believe that people gained a lot of weight over the holidays. Everything seemed to be perfect, and how could anything ever change that? But life is not always perfect.

The day after Christmas when everyone had just sat down to breakfast, Trent suddenly turned ashen.

"I feel funny. My arm doesn't feel right, and I'm feeling dizzy."

Without warning he toppled out of his chair and fell onto the floor. Joby was the first one to reach his side.

"Call for help!" he shouted.

Duane knelt next to him to see if he could feel a pulse and detected a very faint one. He immediately started CPR while they were waiting for an ambulance. The paramedics took charge of the situation when they arrived, putting an oxygen mask on Trent and loading him into the ambulance. Carol went with him while Duane took Joby and Davy to the hospital in his car. Unfortunately, they had to go to Sacramento, as the clinic in Rhodes was not equipped to handle such a serious case. That took extra time that they could not afford. Trent was still alive but barely when they reached the hospital in

Sacramento. Doctors there saw immediately that he had suffered a catastrophic heart attack and had little hope he would recover. Early that afternoon the unthinkable happened, and Trent was pronounced dead just a month shy of what would have been his twentieth birthday. How could this have happened to one so young and who seemed to be in excellent health? Duane and Carol were overwhelmed with grief and consented to an autopsy which showed that unbeknownst to them Trent had been born with a heart defect which his doctors had never picked up on, as he never had any murmur. Davy had no idea of what was going on; all he knew is that his parents were crying which made him cry too. Joby asked if he could go in alone and see Trent. He slowly approached the bed where Trent was lying looking as if he were just asleep. He gently touched Trent's face and then his own. Then he touched Trent's hand and then his own. Last of all he placed his hand over Trent's heart and then over his own and whispered the word, "Same."

The young nurse in the room covered her face as tears started running down her cheeks, but Joby's eyes remained dry. He turned and walked out of the room without saying another word.

Several days passed after they returned home, and Joby said very little, remaining mostly silent. He had no appetite, and Dean tried his best to encourage him to eat. He suspected that Joby was in shock. None of the housemates had as yet returned from spending the holidays with their families, so it was just the two of them there now. One afternoon Dean left to do some grocery shopping and couldn't persuade Joby to join him. He was concerned about leaving him alone, but he had no choice. After Dean left, Joby wandered aimlessly throughout the house, ending up in the living room. Suddenly he noticed a bible lying on a small table, and without warning the floodgates opened. Joby snatched the bible off the table and began ripping pages out of it, screaming and sobbing.

"Why did you take my best friend?" he wailed. "Why not me?

Why Trent? I should have been the one. I hate you for this. I hope you go to hell and stay there. You don't belong in heaven. What kind of a god would do this?"

He sat on the floor until he had ripped out all of the pages, his whole-body trembling and shaking with sobs. At last exhausted, he curled himself up into a fetal position surrounded by sheets of paper.

When Dean arrived home about an hour later, the place was very quiet. He walked into the living room, and there was Joby with a roll of scotched tape trying to mend something, struggling to do so with his compromised hands. Dean immediately saw they were pages from a bible.

"I c can't g get it b back t together," Joby sobbed.

His eyes were almost swollen shut, and mucus was pouring out of both nostrils, dripping over his lips and onto his shirt. Dean knelt beside him and gently took hold of both his hands.

"Joby stop. You don't have to put it back together."

"Yes, I do. I told God to go to hell and that I hated him. Now he will hate me."

"God doesn't hate you, Joby. He loves you even more because He sees what pain you are in. I don't know why God took Trent, but I do know that He had a reason, and in time you will learn what it is. He has a purpose for doing everything no matter how difficult that may be for us. I'm convinced he left you here for a purpose."

When he saw that Joby was too spent to stand, he lifted him up in his arms, carried him upstairs and laid him on his bed. He took a cool rag and gently washed his face. He removed Joby's shoes and covered him with a blanket. Joby turned on his side and immediately fell asleep. I guess you could say this was Joby's catharsis. It was the start of him beginning to heal and accept Trent's death.

PART 4

A Search for Purpose

Purpose Revealed

Several weeks after Trent's untimely death, Dean took a call from Duane asking if he could speak to Joby. He immediately called Joby to the phone. Duane said they would be having a memorial service for Trent at the end of the month and wondered if Joby would feel up to giving the eulogy. Joby was glad that Duane could not see the tears rolling down his cheeks. He said he would be extremely honored to do so and would be looking forward to seeing him as well as Carol and Davy in the near future.

Dean drove Joby on the long trip to Rhodes where the Hardings were waiting for him in front of their place. Joby left the car and immediately hugged each one of the them.

"I can't tell you how honored I am that you asked me to do this. Trent was my best friend in the entire world, and I know he would want me to do this," said Joby.

"There is no doubt in my mind either," replied Duane.

The day of the memorial service arrived. It was scheduled on Friday at 10 a.m. Joby was wearing a black suit that Dean had bought for him along with a dark gray shirt and black tie. He was also wearing a new pair of black shoes which were fastened with Velcro. Joby had difficulty tying laces with his compromised hands, and his shoes were always coming untied. Velcro would eliminate this problem. So many people were expected to attend that the service was being held in the high school gymnasium. Hundreds of chairs were set up clear to the back. The Hardings were seated in the front row near to where a microphone had been set up for Joby's eulogy as well as for any others who might wish to pay tribute to Trent.

When it came time for Joby to speak, he limped

up carrying no notes. His thoughts would come straight from his heart. All eyes were on him, and no one seemed to notice his deformities.

"Trent was my best friend in the whole world. I never had a friend aside from our group home supervisor Dean until Trent came to work there. He was doing community service for something that had happened in his past. From the very beginning Trent accepted me for who I was and not because he felt sorry for me. He always had my back when I was being bullied by the other residents or by the neighborhood kids.

I like to think that Trent felt the same way about me, that he considered me his best friend as well. In a way I think we saved each other. I've also come to know Trent's family. Last Christmas Trent invited me there, and December 25th was the best day of my entire life. Always before I had to be alone in the group home since everyone else was away, aside from Dean. However, December 26th was the worst day, because that was the day I lost my best friend. I will never get over losing Trent, but time has made it a bit easier which is why I was able to come here today. I know you all loved

Trent as well. I don't think he would want us to be sad today. I think he would want us to recall all the good memories we have of him   and move forward with our lives. I'm going to do my best to honor him by doing that, and I hope you will also. Thank you, Trent. I know you are in a good place, and I look forward to seeing you again someday. Until then, rest in peace my beloved friend."

When Joby finished speaking, there was not a dry eye in the room. They saw Joby as being a very special person, and many wished they could be more like him.

Several others spoke after Joby, and the service ended with the hymn, "It is Well With My Soul." Aside from the Hardings and their pastor, only Joby was allowed to be present during the burial. They all shed tears and put their arms around each other as the casket was lowered into the ground. A nice reception followed in the large fellowship hall at the Episcopal church where the Hardings were members. People donated all sorts of finger foods, and everyone who attended spent time reminiscing about the good times they had with Trent.

Davy couldn't understand what had happened to Trent. He spent the following days wandering aimlessly through the house calling out for him. His parents along with Joby tried their best to make him understand, but it was just beyond his comprehension. They hoped in time he would be able to do without Trent, and that day would soon come. His childish mind forgot about his brother, as Joby began to take his place.

Dean knew he would have to return to San Jose soon, but Duane asked him if he could possibly stay in Rhodes a couple of days longer. He said he had something important he wanted to discuss with

89

Joby. Dean agreed, saying what difference could a day or two make. Besides he knew Joby would be sad to say goodbye to the Hardings.

The following morning when Joby came downstairs for what he thought would be his final day there, Duane said something astounding.

"Joby, how would you like to remain here with us forever? We would like to adopt you and make you our son. We know you can't replace Trent, but you would be filling a hole in our lives and helping us move positively forward. We all love you, especially Davy. He would be heartbroken to have you leave us. So how does becoming Joby Harding sound? You are free to think it over if need be. Joby was so overwhelmed that he was speechless. There was nothing to think over. Bursting into tears, he grabbed hold of Duane, hugged him tightly and buried his face on Duane's shoulder.

"I take that it's a yes." All Joby could do was nod his head in the affirmative. He finally would have the family he had always longed for, and to say he was happy was an understatement.

Dean was amazed when he heard the news. This was something Joby had always deserved, and he couldn't be more pleased for him. Joby said he didn't want to return to the group home. He didn't leave anything that really mattered to him there. Dean wished him the best and said what a privilege it had been to know him. Duane told him not to be a stranger and feel free to visit whenever he wanted. Joby gave Dean a hug and thanked him for everything. With that Dean set out for the long drive home.

Shortly after that, Joby decided to volunteer in Davy's special education class. Oddly enough, the students there didn't seem to notice anything strange about his appearance. Like Davy, they were totally accepting of him from day one. They couldn't wait for him to show up each morning and would run up and hug him. The teachers were also grateful for the extra help. He accompanied them on field trips into the community and never minded the stares he got. They no longer mattered to him.

After the adoption was finalized, Duane and Carol decided to try and find a surgeon who might possibly improve Joby's appearance. They found a highly recommended orthopedic one at the UC Davis Medical Center. They realized they probably wouldn't be able to afford this, but thought it was worth a try. They took along a picture of Joby to show to the surgeon since Joby had to remain home to look after Davy. When the surgeon was told what a terrible life Joby had suffered in the past, he agreed to perform the surgery for free. Grateful beyond words, Duane and Carol were convinced that despite there being so many bad individuals, there were still some good ones in the world today.

When the time came for Joby's surgery, all three of them went to the hospital. Carol remained in the waiting room with Davy while Duane and Joby met with the surgeon. The surgeon was even more taken with Joby when meeting him in person. He couldn't have imagined what this young man must have endured given what he looked like. He was scheduled for his first surgery early the following morning and had to fast overnight.

During the first operation, the surgeon rebuilt Joby's nose by giving him a nose bridge and repositioning the nostrils. Joby would now have a normal- looking nose instead of the one he had which resembled a snout. The second surgery proved much more difficult than the first. The surgeon shortened the distance between Joby's nose and mouth and repositioned his lips so his face no longer resembled a canine's muzzle. The final surgeries involved straightening Joby's wrists and ankles so he could use his hands well and walk normally for the first time. The recovery was long, and very painful. However, Joby refused to take any medication, saying the pain he had endured in the past was far worse. This made the surgeon know just how much Joby must have suffered from the terrible abuse he had undergone years ago while in foster care.

When the bandages were finally removed from Joby's face, he was given a mirror to see himself. He never wanted to look at himself in a mirror as he considered himself a freak, but now he didn't recognize himself. Instead of seeing a freak, he saw a handsome young man. Overwhelmed, all he could do was put his hands over his heart and mouth the words, "Thank you," as the tears rolled down his cheeks. There was not a dry eye in the room. Even the surgeon was deeply moved.

The Hardings knew they had to prepare Davy for the change he would see in Joby. He would no longer look like the same person, and they feared how Davy might react. They showed him a picture of Joby beforehand and tried to explain to him that Joby had only changed in appearance; he was still the same person who loved him. They needn't have worried. As soon as Davy saw Joby, he ran up to him and hugged him.

"You pretty, Joby."

"I think you mean handsome. Girls are pretty."
"Right, Joby no girl," said Davy who struggled as usual to get the words out.

Back in Rhodes, people couldn't get over the change in Joby's appearance. With his coal black eyes, long eyelashes, and thick curly black hair he was indeed very handsome. For the first time he went out on a date, taking a girl to the movies and for coffee afterwards. Never did he imagine he would ever do this, and there were other dates following this one. He also started singing in the choir at the Episcopal church where the Hardings attended and where his deep baritone voice was much appreciated.

Joby loved spending time with Davy. He took him to the park, to the movies, and out for burgers and ice cream. He told the Hardings that he would always look after Davy, and they would never need to worry about him after they were gone. For the first time in their married life, Duane and Carol felt a sense of peace.

Joby frequently visited Trent's grave. He would sit there for long periods of time talking to him, convinced that Trent could hear him. He told him how much he missed him and how he was looking forward to seeing him again. One day when he went there it had been raining. Just as he arrived, the sun broke through the clouds, and a beautiful rainbow appeared directly overhead. Suddenly Joby had the answer to the question he had wondered about for so long. It had been there all the time; he had just failed to see it. He knew why he had lived and why Trent had died. He had overcome the suffering he had endured in the past, and like the biblical Job, he was redeemed and rewarded for his faith. God had given him a purpose to fulfill, and he had been doing that all along. He also knew what Trent had met when he said," God works in mysterious ways." He was ready to continue his mission and was very happy to be alive.

At the beginning of each school year Joby gave a talk to both high school and elementary school students about bullying. He said that just because someone doesn't look like you or is handicapped is no reason to bully that person. He knew firsthand how terrible this can be. The kids started taking this to heart, and it became far less of a problem. When word got around, Joby was asked to give the same talk at other schools in the area. He also wrote a book called, "*A Life of Job*", which became a best seller. He never stopped fulfilling his purpose which he considered to be a gift from God.

Perhaps this gift was never more on display than when there was a horrendous accident during foggy weather on the interstate going through the Central Valley. More than a hundred cars and trucks slammed into each other, and many overturned blocking both sides of the freeway.

Ten people were killed and dozens more were injured, many critically. Some ended up in the hospital in Sacramento, and when Joby heard about this, he immediately went there. He visited all the injured, especially the children where he held their hands and wiped away their tears. He also brought a gift to each one of them. He told them how years ago when he was just ten, the only two people who had ever loved him and who were planning to adopt him were killed in an automobile accident. He couldn't understand why a loving God would do such a thing. However, a few years later his life took a different direction when he would meet someone who would totally change his life. It was then he learned that God had given him a special purpose to fulfill, and he felt forever blessed. Years later he heard back from one of these children saying he had read Joby's book and heard him speak. His life had also been blessed despite losing both of his parents.

There were many other times when Joby's life made an impact on others, and he forever thanked God for giving him the purpose to do this. As a result, he made the world a better place.

A Search for Purpose

Epilogue

Over the years, Rhodes more than doubled in size. Many came from the Bay Area fed up with the high cost of housing and the nightmarish traffic. They didn't mind the summer heat as long as they had air-conditioning. Plus, it was just a short drive to Sacramento where some worked in the defense industry, and the commute was worth it. A computer company moved to Rhodes, and a number of software engineers came there to work which helped to put Rhodes on the map.

Musicians moved there and eventually formed the Rhodes Symphony which performed concerts in a newly built theater. Artists also came, and soon an art gallery was built. When the citizens decided that they need to preserve Rhodes' history, they built a small museum. The old movie theater was torn down, and a brand new one was erected in its place. The small medical clinic was enlarged bringing more doctors and nurses so people were not always stuck going to Sacramento for treatment. A large shopping mall sprang up with some high-end stores as did some more exclusive restaurants. No longer were there just fast-food places and the pizza parlor. Many of the new arrivals were Democrats, so Rhodes became a two- party town, making for some rather lively political debates.

Joby never married, although there were a number of women interested in him. However, he knew they wanted children, and he never wanted to father a child who might inherit whatever caused his strange condition. However, at age 40 he was finally able to experience the joy of having sex with an older woman who had reached menopause. They met a few more times before she left the area to be closer to relatives. After that he maintained a platonic relationship with a woman named Amy Bowers. They enjoyed spending time together going to restaurants and movies. Because they both loved music, they always bought season tickets to the Rhodes Symphony. They also traveled together, making several trips abroad. They especially enjoyed Paris with its unique architecture. He never forgot the words Trent spoke to him long ago when he said one never knows what God may have in store for them. He never imagined back then how much he would be rewarded in the future.

Sally always regretted putting distance between herself and Trent after the abortion. He was her first love, and he deserved better. She also never got over the guilt about having the abortion. If she had known beforehand that her parents would forgive her as well as forgive Trent, she never would have had it in the first place. They told her nothing she could ever do would stop them from loving her, including this. She was terribly saddened by Trent's death, but she knew she had to move forward beyond her grief and forge a new life. She married a young software engineer named Eric Taylor who

103

worked at the computer company. Sally told her husband before they wed about the abortion, as she didn't want to keep any secrets from him. Eric wrapped her in his arms and told her that nothing could stop him from loving her.

Sally made a beautiful bride and asked Eric's sister to be her maid of honor. She told Joby that she had dreaded going to Trent's memorial service, but in the end, she was very glad she did. Just hearing Joby speak about his friendship with Trent and not being able to say goodbye to him when he passed away made Sally realize that she and Joby had something in common. Sally also never had a chance to say goodbye to Trent. Joby said he knew in his heart that Trent forgave her for shunning him, and that gave her a sense of peace. Eric had come to know Joby from what Sally had told him about him. Consequently, he asked Joby to be his best man as he had so much admiration for him. He would be the brother to him that he never had, as he had just his one sister. The church was packed, and afterwards there was a wonderful reception in the large parish hall. Sally and Eric honeymooned in Hawaii and later moved into a large home on the outskirts of Rhodes. They eventually had two children, a boy and a girl. They asked Joby to be their godfather, and he was honored to do so. Many years later, Sally and Eric would be blessed with several grandchildren, and Joby took great delight in being part of their lives also and having them call him "Grandpa Joby."

Sadly, one morning years earlier, the Hardings found Davy had died in his sleep due to an unforeseen heart defect which was often common in those with Down's syndrome. It was devastating for both Duane and Carol and also for Joby. However, Joby took comfort in knowing that Davy was now well and in a far better place where he was enjoying his favorite burgers and ice cream. He was buried next to Trent in the local cemetery, and the three of them always placed fresh flowers on both graves on Memorial Day.

Joby continued to make good on fulfilling his purpose. As word spread, he was asked to speak at places all over the country, and he was always pleased to do so. It was his way of trying to make a difference and being an advocate for all disabled people. He considered this to be his mission in life.

He also kept another promise he had made years ago which was to look after Duane and Carol when they were no longer able to do so themselves. Many years later he moved in with them and served as their caregiver right up until the end. They both passed away in their late 80s, within just a few weeks from each other after being married for over 60 years. They were buried next to their two sons, Trent Addison Harding and David Benjamin Harding. Joby knew that one day he would be put to rest there also, and he felt at peace knowing that.

By then Joby was in his mid-60s. He was still a

handsome man even though his coal black hair was now completely gray. He stood ramrod straight which showed he was aging well. He and his long-time friend, Amy, continued to enjoy their time together. For a while they discussed marriage, but in the end decided to keep things the way they were. Amy's chestnut hair was now totally silver, and she was a bit more matronly than she was when she and Joby first met, while Joby still retained his slim form. Now that they were older, they preferred going on cruises.

They enjoyed a trip to Alaska on an ocean cruise, where they marveled at seeing the glaciers and visited a sled dog site. They took the train to Denali and were fortunate to see Mt. Denali on a fair day with its snow-capped peak. They also took a river cruise down the Seine in France and visited the beaches of Normandy where the allied forces went ashore in terrible weather during World War Two. It was such a beautiful day when they were there, that it was hard to imagine what it must have been like on D-Day back in 1944 when the Allied troops came to shore in stormy weather. They visited the graves and were given a red rose to place on one of them. If Joby had ever known what his life would be like many years later, he would not have believed it. God had rewarded him greatly, and for that he would be forever thankful.

Joby's life was always one of purpose. It was the reason he was born, and he always felt fulfilled because of it.

One of his favorite verses came from a poem by Robert Frost.

"The woods are lovely, dark and deep. But I have promises to keep and miles to go before I sleep."

Joby knew he needed to continue fulfilling his purpose. Many years later he passed away in his sleep at age 90. He was buried next to the other Hardings in the family plot, and the inscription on his tombstone would read, "A life well lived."

Acknowledgments

I want to give tremendous thanks to Theresa Jennetti for editing my book and to Karl Kadie for making some valuable content suggestions and for writing a nice tribute on the back cover. I also want to thank Carol Korzow and Alison Sheaf who have read the book and expressed great compliments. I am also deeply grateful for my husband, Tony, who has always supported me no matter what the cause. Finally, I owe thanks to our writers group in Eureka for inspiring me to write this.

About the Author

MJ Jennetti graduated from Ohio State University, where she majored in English. After teaching briefly at the secondary level, she spent most of her career working in special education. She is also the author of *Painting With Poetry, A Poetic Memoir*. She lives in Eureka, California.

Discussion Questions

1. How does the book illustrate the importance of facing mental health illness?

2. What difference might it have made if Trent and Sally had told their parents about the pregnancy?

3. How does the book show that God works in mysterious ways?

4. How might Joby's life have been different if Trent had lived?

5. What important lesson did Joby teach Trent and how did his method differ from Sally's?

6. When Joby went on field trips with Davy's class, why do you suppose the stares he got from people no longer bothered him?

7. Discuss some of the ways Joby fulfilled his purpose.

8. What important event in the book is illustrated on the cover?

9. What promises did Joby keep to the Hardings?

10. Do you think this book could be appreciated by people of all faiths?

11. How did the book affect you personally?

www.ingramcontent.com/pod-product-compliance
Lightning Source LLC
Chambersburg PA
CBHW060334260626
47160CB00007B/2790